THE POWER OF PRAYER
BY

Max Brand

FOREWORD

Max Brand was an American author best known for writing Western fiction.

The Power of Prayer

I. — WHEN WEST MEETS EAST

One could not say that it was love of one's native country which brought Gerald home again. It would be more accurate to say that it was the only country where his presence did not create too much heat for comfort. In the past ten years, forty nations—no less—had been honored by the coming of Gerald and had felt themselves still more blessed, perhaps, by his departure unannounced. Into the history of forty nations he had written his name, and now he was come back to the land and the very region of his birth.

No matter if the police of Australia breathed deeply and ground their teeth at the thought of him; no matter if the sleuths of France spent spare hours pouring over photographs of that lean and handsome face, swearing to themselves that under any disguise he would now be recognized; no matter if an Arab sheik animated his cavalry by recounting the deeds of Gerald; no matter if a South American republic held up its million hands in thanksgiving that the firebrand had fallen upon another land; no matter were all these things and more, now that the ragged tops of the Rocky Mountains had swept past the train which bore him westward.

When he dismounted at a nameless town and drew a deep breath of the thin, pure, mountain air, he who had seen forty nations swore to himself that the land which bore him was the best of all.

He had been fourteen when he left the West. But sixteen years could by no means dim the memories of his childhood. For was not this the very land where he had learned to ride and to shoot? A picture of what he had been rushed upon his memory—a fire-eyed youngster with flaming red hair, riding anything on four feet on the range, fighting with hard-knuckled fists, man or boy, delving deep into the mysteries of guns, baffling his very brother with lies, the cunning depth of which were like the bottomless sea.

He smiled as he remembered. No one would know him now. The fire-red had altered to dark auburn. The gleam was banished from his eyes, saving on occasion! And the ragged urchin could never be seen in this dapper figure clad in whipcord riding breeches and mounted—oh, hardy gods of the Far West behold him!—in a flat English saddle.

But, for the nonce, an English saddle pleased him. Time was when he had made himself at home in a wild Tartar's saddle on a wild Tartar horse, emptying his carbine at the yelling pursuers—but that was another picture, and that was another day. For the present he was happier encased in a quiet and easy manner of soft-spoken gentility. It was the manner which this morning he had slipped into as another man slips into a coat. And for ten years, to do on the spur of the moment what the moment made him desire to do, had been religion with Gerald.

To be sure, when he came down to breakfast in that outfit and ate his bread and drank his coffee in the little dingy hotel dining room, people stared at him. But Gerald was not unaccustomed to being the cynosure of neighboring eyes.

Then he went forth to buy a horse, and the dealer, after a glance at those riding breeches, led forth a high-headed bay, with much profane commendation and a high price. But Gerald, in a voice as smooth as a hand running over silk, pointed out that the beast was bone-spavined and declined with thanks. And so he went on from horse to horse. But it seemed that his glance went through each beast like a sword of fire. One look, and he knew the worst that could be said of it. The horse dealer followed, sweating with discomfort, until Gerald pointed to a distant corral with a single dark-chestnut mare standing in it.

"That yonder," he said, "that one yonder, my friend, looks as though it might be for me."

The dealer glanced at the little English saddle which all this time Gerald carried over the crook of his arm.

"I'll saddle her for you in a minute," he said. "Yep. You picked the winner. I'd hate to see Sorrow go, but for a price I guess it could be fixed."

"Why is she called Sorrow?" said Gerald.

"Because she's got sad eyes," said the horse dealer and looked Gerald calmly in the face.

So the little English pad was placed on Sorrow, and she was led out, gentle-mannered as a lamb, until the rider dropped into his place. That jarring weight transformed Sorrow into a vivid semblance of dynamite exploding.

"She busted herself in sixteen directions all at once," said the horse dealer afterward. "And, when she went the sixteenth way, this fellow stopped follering. He sailed about a mile and landed on his head. I came over on the run. I sure thought his neck was broke. But he was on his feet before I got to him. And the light of fighting fire was in his eye. He up and jumped onto that mare in no time. Well, she sun-fished and she bucked and she reared, and did she shake him this time? Not a bit of it! He stuck like a cactus bur. And after she'd tried her last trick, she realized she had an unbeatable master, and she quieted down like a pet kitten. He rode her away as if she had been raised by him and ridden by him for years."

Which was the truth. Sorrow stepped high and pretty, albeit obediently, back to the hotel. Here Gerald left her at the hitch rack while he threaded his way through the group of loungers on the porch and went in to freshen his appearance. In a few minutes he came downstairs whistling. On the front verandah he spoke to the first comer, and the first comer was Harkey, the big blacksmith.

"What is there to see around here?" he asked of Harkey. "Can you tell me of any points of interest?"

Harkey stared at him, and all he could see was the whipcord riding trousers and the tailor-made cigarette which drawled from a corner of Gerald's mouth.

"I dunno," said Harkey. "There ain't nothing that I've seen around here that would match up with you as a point of interest!"

And he laughed heartily at his good jest, and along the verandah the loungers took up the laughter in a long chorus.

"My friend," said Gerald gently, "you seem to me to be a trifle impertinent."

"The devil I do," said Harkey.

"But no doubt," said Gerald, "you can explain."

"Me?" said Harkey, and he balled his sooty fists.

"Yes," said Gerald, "you."

"I'll see you and ten of your kind in hell first," said Harkey.

"My dear fellow," said Gerald, "how terribly violent you are!"

And with that he stepped six inches forward with his left foot and struck with his left hand, swift as an arrow off the string, deadly as a barbed spear driven home. Vain were those thick muscles which cushioned the base of Harkey's jaw. The knuckles bit through them to the bone, and the shock, hammer-like, jarred his brain. The great knees of Harkey bent under him, benumbed. He slipped inert to the ground, his back against a supporting pillar, and Gerald turned to the rest.

"I have been asking," he said, "for the points of interest around the town. Can any of you tell me?"

They looked upon the fallen body of Harkey; they stared into the dead eyes of the giant; they regarded his sagging jaw; and they were inspired to speak. Yonder among the mountains, due north and a scant fifty miles away, where the Culver River had gouged for itself a trench, gold had been found, they said, not many months before. And in the town of Culver there would be points of interest, they said. Yes, there would be many points of interest for one who wished to see the West.

When his back was turned, they smiled to one another. No doubt this fellow was a man of some mark. There lay the body of Harkey, now showing the first quivering signs of life. And yonder was he of the whipcord riding breeches mounted upon famous Sorrow, famous Sorrow now dancing down the road with her first-found master. But in spite of these things, what would happen when Gerald reached Culver City, where the great men of the West were gathered? He might ride a horse as well as the next man. He might crush the slow-handed blacksmith with one cunning blow. But what would be his ventures among those men of might, those deadly warriors who fairly thought a gun out of the holsters and smote an enemy with an inescapable lightning flash?

Such were the thoughts of the wise men as they shifted their quids and rolled fresh cigarettes, but among them all there was not one guessed the truth, that the West was meeting the West as

Greek meets Greek.

Even wiser men than they might have been baffled, seeing those daintily tailored trousers, those shop-made cigarettes each neatly monogrammed, and the high-stirruped, slippery saddle in which he sat. For who could have told that the same West which had fathered them in overalls and chaps and bandannas had fathered this returned prodigal also?

II. — GERALD GOES TO CULVER CITY

But Gerald knew. Ah, yes, Gerald knew, and the knowledge was as sweet to him as is the sight of a marked card to an expert gambler. Why had he roamed so long away from them? This, after all, was his country, in which he was to carve his destiny. Let Paris keep her laughing boulevards and Monte Carlo the blueness of her sea—these raw-headed mountains, these hard-handed men, spelled home to Gerald. What mattered it if, in his wallet, there was a scant fifty dollars, his all of worldly wealth, so long as there was a gun at his hip, smoke in his nostrils, and beneath him a horse that went as sweetly as a song?

Up the valley he wound and, topping the first range, he looked down on a pitching sea of peaks. Somewhere among them was gold. Yes, due north from him he would find gold, and wherever there was gold there was electric excitement thrilling in the air. Wherever there was gold, there were sure to be lovely women with clever tongues and brave men with hands of iron and other men with wits as keen as the glimmering edge of a Damascus blade. That was no meaningless simile to one who had learned saber play—and used it!

It was the dull time of the evening when he came in view of Culver City. The double-jacks and the single-jacks were no longer ringing in the valley. But up the valley road the teamster was still cursing his twelve mules to a faster walk, and up the valley road other men were coming on horseback or in old caravan wagons, a steady stream typical of that which flowed into Culver City all day and every day and never flowed out again. What became of them, then, since the city never grew beyond a certain size? That was an easy riddle. Superfluous life was needed. It was needed to be ground away in the mines which pock-marked with pools of shadow the valley here and there; it was needed still more to feed into the mill which ground out pleasure in the gaming halls and the dance halls in Culver City.

Gerald was new to mining camps. What he knew of the West was the West of the cow country, the boundless cattle ranges. But, with knowing one bit of the West, all the rest lies beyond an open door at the most. He who has burned the back of his neck in the sun and roped his cow and ridden out his blizzard, can claim knowledge of the open sesame which unlocks a thousand mysteries. So Gerald looked down upon the new scene with the feeling that he almost knew the men whom he would find strolling through the long, crooked street of Culver City.

And know them he did, though not out of his knowledge of the West. He had seen all their faces before. He had seen them gather around the standard of that delightful revolution which had budded south of Panama and almost made him a famous man. He had seen them in politer garb around the gaming tables of the full forty nations. He had seen them hither and yon gathering like bees around honey wherever danger and hope went hand in hand.

But of course he had never seen one of them before. He was as safe under his true name in this little town as though he wore the most complicated alias and barbered disguise in Paris. And, ah, what a joy it was to be able to ride with eyes straightforward and no fear of who might come beside him or who from behind. Here in his own country, his home country, he was safe at last. He watched the yellow lights begin to burn out from the hollow as the evening thickened. And not a face on which those lights were now shining knew any ill of him!

He began to breathe more freely. He began to raise his head. Why not start life all anew? Hither and yon and here and there he had felt that life had pursued him through the world, and he had had no chance to settle down to labor and honesty. Now, however, he was quite free from controlling circumstance. He could carve his own destiny.

What if his capital were only honest resolution plus just a trifle more of capital than fifty dollars? Should he not spend one night at the gaming tables before he entered the sphere of the law-abiding, the law-reverent?

Sorrow had been going smoothly down the slope all this while. None like Sorrow to pick a way among the boulders, none like Sorrow to come through the rough going with never a shock and never a jar for her rider. And that day the mare had traveled farther into the land of knowledge than her rider had traveled into the mountains. She had learned that a human voice may be pleasantly low and steady; she had learned that a bit may be a helpful guide and not a torture instrument to tear her mouth; she had learned, for the mind of a man comes down the firm rein and telegraphs its thought into the brain of a horse. It was all very wonderful and all very strange.

A door slammed nearby. In the morning Sorrow would have leaped to the side first and turned to look afterward. But now she merely pricked her short, sharp ears. It was a girl singing in the door of a cabin, with the soft, yellow light of a lantern curving over arms which were bare to the elbow and glowing in her hair. Sorrow stopped short. In the old days of colthood and pasture and carelessness before she began the long battle against man, there had been even such a girl who would come to the pasture bars with a whistle which meant apples were waiting.

As for Gerald, he came on the view of the girl at that very moment when his thought was turning back toward the gaming tables and the necessary capital with which one might launch forth on a career of honesty.

"Good evening," he called.

"Hello," said the girl. "Tommy dear, is that you?"

Gerald frowned. Who was "Tommy dear?" At any rate, though at that moment she moved so that the light struck clearly along her profile, he decided that he did not wish to linger.

"No," he said dryly, "this is not Tommy."

A touch on the reins, and Sorrow fled swiftly down the valley toward the place where the lights thickened, and from which the noise was drifting up. So he came into Culver City at a gallop, with a singular anger filling him, a singular desire to find Tommy and discover what manner of man he might be.

In the meantime, he must have a room. He went to that strange and staggering building known as the hotel. In the barn behind it he put up Sorrow in a commodious stall and saw that she was well fed. Then he entered the hotel itself.

He had quite forgotten that his garb was not the ordinary costume for Culver City and its mines. The minute he stepped into the flare of the lanterns which lighted the lobby of the hotel, he was greeted with a murmur and then a half-stifled guffaw which warned him that he was an outlander to these fellows. And Gerald paused and looked about him.

Ordinarily, he would have passed on as though he were deaf. But now his mind was filled with the memory of those rounded arms of the girl at the cabin door, and how the lights had glimmered softly about her lips and chin, and how she had smiled as she called to him. Who was "Tommy dear?"

It made Gerald very angry. So he stopped just inside the door of the hotel and looked about him, letting his glance rest on every face, one by one. And every face was nothing to him but a blur, so great was his anger and so sharply was he still seeing the girl at the cabin door. He drew out a cigarette case. It was solidest gold. And a jeweler in Vienna had done the chasing which covered it. A millionaire had bought it for a huge sum. And the millionaire had given the case to Gerald for the sake of a little story which Gerald told on an evening—a little story hardly ten words long. From that gleaming case he extracted his monogrammed cigarette. He lighted his smoke. And then he shut the case and bestowed it in his coat pocket once more, while the laughter which had been spreading from a murmur to a chuckle, suddenly burst out in a roar from one man's throat.

It was Red Charlie. He stood in the center of the room. Above his head was the circular platform around which the four lanterns hung—a platform some three or four feet wide and suspended by a single wire from the ceiling above. But Red Charlie laughed almost alone. The others preferred to swallow the major portion of their mirth for there was that about the dapper stranger which discouraged insult. The slow and methodical way in which he had looked from face to face, for instance, had been a point worth noting.

But Charlie could afford laughter. He had made his strike a week before, had sold his mine three days later, and he was now in the fourth stage of growing mellow. The more he laughed, the more heavy was the silence which spread through the room. And suddenly the laughter of Charlie went out, for there is a physical force in silence. It presses in upon the mind. And Charlie palled himself together. The fumes of liquor were swept from his brain. He became cold sober in a trice, facing the slender figure of Gerald.

"I love a good joke," said the quiet voice of Gerald. "Won't someone tell me the point?"

There was no reply.

"I love a good joke," repeated Gerald. "And you, my friend, were laughing very loudly."

It was too pointed for escape. Red Charlie swelled himself to anger.

"There's only one point in sight," he said. "And you're it, stranger."

"Really?" said Gerald. "Then I'm sorry to say that, much as I enjoy a good jest, I detest being laughed at. But of course you are sorry for the slip?"

"Sorry?" said Red Charlie.

He blinked at the stranger and then grasped the butt of a gun. Had a life of labor been spent in vain? Had he not built a sufficient reputation? Was he to be challenged by every chance tenderfoot?

"Why, damn your eyes," exploded Charlie and whipped out his weapon.

Be it said for Charlie that he intended only to splinter the floor with his bullets so that he and his friends might enjoy the exquisite pleasure of seeing the stranger hop about for safety which existed only outside the door. In all his battles it could never be said that Charlie had turned a gun upon an unarmed man.

But now a weapon was conjured into the hand of the stranger. It winked out into view. It exploded. At the same instant the taut wire which held the platform and the lanterns snapped with a twanging sound. Down rushed platform and all and crashed upon the head of Red Charlie. Down went Charlie in a terrible mass of wreckage.

And Gerald walked on to write his name in the register. His back was turned when the platform was raised and Charlie was lifted to his feet. But as for Charlie, all thought of battle had left him. Mild and chastened of spirit, he stole softly through the door.

III. — TOMMY DEAR

Two things were pointed out afterward—first, that the oddly attired stranger who wrote the name of Gerald Kern on the register had not lingered to enjoy the comments of the bystanders; and, second, it was noted that the wire which he had cut with his bullet was no more than a glimmering ray of light, though he had severed it with a snap shot from the hip.

The second observation carried with it many corollaries. For instance, it was made plain that this dexterous gunfighter would maintain his personal dignity at all costs, but it was equally apparent that he did not wish to shed human blood. Otherwise, he would have made no scruple of shooting through the head a man who had already drawn a weapon. Furthermore, he had quelled a bully and done it in a fashion which would furnish Culver City with an undying jest, and Culver City appreciated a joke.

And when Gerald came downstairs that evening he found that the town was ready to receive him with open arms. Which developed this difficulty, that Gerald was by no means ready to be embraced. He kept the honest citizens of Culver City at arm's length. And so he came eventually to the gaming hall of Canton Douglas. A long residence in the Orient and an ability to chatter with the Chinese coolies accounted for the nickname. It might also have been held to account for the gaming passion in Douglas.

But he was famous for the honesty of his policy even more than for his love of chance. Gerald, the moment he stepped inside the doors of the place, recognized that he was in the domain of a gamester of the first magnitude. And he looked about him with a hungry eye.

Here was all that he could wish for. One glance assured him that the place was square. A second glance told him that the stakes were running mountain high, for these gamblers had dug their gold raw out of the ground, and they were willing to throw it away as though it were so much dirt. Gerald saw a thousand dollars won on the turn of a card and then turned his back resolutely on the place and faced the open door through which new patrons were streaming. The good resolve was still strong as iron in him. The clean life and the free life still beckoned him on! And, with a heart which rose high with the sense of his virtue, he had almost reached the door when he heard some one calling from the side.

"Hello, Tommy!" said the voice. "Here's your place. Better luck tonight!"

Gerald turned to see what this Tommy might be, and he found a fellow in the late twenties, tall, strong, handsome, a veritable ideal of all that a man should be in outward appearance. But there was a promise of something more than mere good looks in him. There was a steadiness in his blue eyes that Gerald liked, and he had the frank and ready smile of one who has nothing to conceal from the world.

He knew in a thrice that this was the "Tommy dear" of the girl. And Gerald paused—paused to take out his cigarette case and begin another smoke. In reality, he was lingering to watch the other man more closely. And how could he linger so near without being invited?

"We need five to make up a good game," the dealer for Canton Douglas was saying. "Where's a fifth? You, Alex? Sit in, Hamilton? Then what about you, stranger?"

Four faces turned suddenly upon Gerald.

After all, he said to himself, he would make a point of not winning. He would make a point of rising from the table with exactly the same amount with which he sat down.

"I'll be very happy to sit in," said Gerald. He paused behind his chair. "My name is Kern, gentlemen," he said.

They blundered to their feet, gave their names, shook hands with him; as he touched each hand he knew by the awe in their eyes that they had heard the tale of the breaking of the wire in the hotel. Nay, they had heard even more, for the news of the riding of Sorrow and the encounter with Harkey had followed him as the wake follows the ship. After all, Harkey was a known man for the weight of his fists, and scientific boxing seems always miraculous to the uninitiated.

So Gerald sat down facing Tommy Vance, and the game began. As for the cards and the game itself, Gerald gave them only a tithe of his attention. They were younglings, these fellows. Not in years to be sure, but their experience compared with his was as that of the newborn babe to the seer of three score and ten. Even Canton Douglas's dealer was a child. In the course of three hands, Gerald knew them all. In the course of six hands, he could begin to tell within a shade of the truth what each man held, and automatically he regulated his betting in accordance. In spite of himself, he was winning, and twice he had to throw money away on worthless hands to keep his stack of chips down to modest proportions.

In the meantime, he was studying Tommy Vance. And what barbed every glance and every thought he gave to Tommy was the picture of the girl in the cabin door. It was odd how closely she lingered in his mind. The ring of her voice seemed always just around the corner in his memory. Through the shadow on her face, he still looked back to her smile. And why under heaven, he asked himself, did he dwell so much on her? There had been other women in the past ten years. There had been a score of them, and not one had really mattered. But when he paused on that dark hillside, it seemed that the door of his soul had been open and the girl had stepped inside.

So he watched every move of Tommy Vance, for every move of a man at a poker game means something. What better test of a man's generosity or steady nerve or careless good nature or venomous malice or envy or wild courage? And the more he saw of Tommy the more good there was in him, and the more dread grew like the falling of a shadow in Gerald.

Men who have seen much evil, and stained their hands with it, are still more sensitive to all that is good. They scent it afar. And all that Gerald saw of big Tom Vance was truest steel. He gambled like a boy playing tag, whole-heartedly, carelessly. When the strong cards were in his hand, how could he keep the mischievous light out of his blue eyes? And yet when his hand was strongest and one of the five had been driven to the wall, Gerald saw him push up the betting and then lay down his cards.

It was a small thing, but it meant much in the eyes of Gerald. He prided himself on his manner and his courtesy, but here was a gentleman by the grace of heaven, and by contrast Gerald felt small and low indeed!

Then Tommy Vance pushed back his chair.

"I've dropped enough to make it square for me to draw out, fellows?" he asked.

"You're not leaving, Tommy?" asked the dealer earnestly. "If you go, the snap is out of the game."

"There's another game for Tommy," and a hard-handed miner chuckled on Gerald's right. "She's waiting for you now, I guess. Is that right, Tommy?"

And Tommy flushed to the eyes, then laughed with a frankness and a happiness that sent a pang of pain through the heart of Gerald.

"She's waiting, Lord bless her," he said.

"Then hurry," said the dealer, "before another fellow steps in and takes up her time."

"Her time?" said Tommy, throwing up his head. "Her time? Boys, there ain't another like her. She's truer than steel and better than gold. She's—"

He checked himself as though realizing that this was no place for pouring forth encomiums on the lady of his heart.

"This breaks up the game, and I'm leaving," said Gerald, rising in turn.

"Are you going up the hill?" said Tommy Vance eagerly.

"I'll walk a step or two with you," said Gerald.

They walked out together into the night, and as they passed down the hall Gerald felt many eyes drawn after him. Yes, it was very plain that all Culver City had heard of his adventures. But now they were out under the stars. Not even the stars which burn low over the wide horizon of the Sahara seemed as bright to Gerald as this heaven above his home mountains.

"Now that we're out here alone," said Vance, "I don't mind telling you what everybody else in Culver City is thinking... that was pretty neat the way you handled Red Charlie. That hound has been barking up every tree that held a fight in it. The town will be a pile quieter now that he's gone. Only, how in the name of the devil did you have the nerve to take a chance with that wire?"

"How in the same name," answered Gerald quietly, "were you induced to lay down that hand of yours which must have been a full house at least... that hand you bet on up to fifty dollars and then laid down to the fellow on my right?"

"Ah?" laughed Tommy Vance. "You knew that? Well, you must be able to look through the backs of the cards. It was a full house, right enough. Three queens on a pair of nines. It looked like money in the bank. But I saw that I'd break poor old Hampton. And that would have spoiled his fun for the evening."

"You're rich in happiness, then," said Gerald. "A good time for every one when you're so happy yourself, eh?"

"Yes," and Tom Vance nodded. "I feel as though my hands were full of gold... a treasure that can't be exhausted. And... well, I won't tire you out talking about a girl you've never seen! But Jack Parker brought her into the talk, you know," he apologized.

"I like to hear you," said Gerald. "It's an old story, perhaps. But what interests me is that every fellow always feels that he is writing chapter one of a new book. I remember hearing a man who was about to marry for the third time. By the Lord, he was as enthusiastic as you. It's the eternal illusion, I suppose. A man cannot help thinking, when he's in love, that a woman will be true and faithful... pure as the snow, true as steel. That's the way of it." And he chuckled softly.

It was entirely a forced laugh, and from the corner of his eye he was studying the effect of his talk upon Tommy Vance. He was studying him as the scientist studies the insect and its wriggling under the prick of the needle and the acid. And certainly Tommy Vance was hard hit.

By his scowl and the outthrust of his lower jaw, Gerald gathered that his companion would have fought sooner than submit to such observations as these had they been made in other than the most casual and good-natured manner.

"You sort of figure," said Tommy Vance, "that women are pretty apt to... pretty apt to..."

He was stuck for words.

"I hate to generalize on such a subject," said Gerald. "Every idiot talks wisely about women. But a man in love is a blind man. He wakens sometimes in a short period. Sometimes he stays blind until he dies. But I never see a pretty girl that I don't think of the spider, so full of wiles... and such instinctive wiles. She can't help smiling in a certain way which you and I both know. And that smile is like dynamite. It's a destructive force. Am I not right, Vance?"

So saying, he clapped his companion lightly on the shoulder, and Vance turned a wan smile upon him. It was delightful to be treated so familiarly by one who had so lately made himself a hero in the town. But still the brow of Tommy was clouded.

"Maybe there's something in what you say," he admitted. "But still, as far as Kate Maddern is concerned, I'd swear..."

His voice stumbled away to nothing.

"Your lady?" said Gerald gaily, forcing his casual tone with the most perfect artistry. "Of course she's the exception. She would be true to you if there were an ocean and ten years between you!"

But here Tommy Vance came to an abrupt halt and faced Gerald, and the latter knew, with a leaping heart, that he was succeeding better than he had ever dreamed he could.

IV. — VANCE MAKES A BET

"Look here" said Vance, "of course I know you're talking about womenfolk in general, but every time you speak like that I keep seeing Kate's face, and it's uncomfortable."

Oh, jealous heart of a lover! Masked by the black of night, Gerald smiled with satisfaction. How fast the fish was rising to the bait!

"As I said before," said Gerald, "I haven't her in mind at all. She's all that you dream of her, of course."

"That's just talk... just words," said Tommy Vance. "Between you and me, you think she's most apt to be like the rest."

"If you wish to pin me down..."

"Kern," said Vance, "if I was to go away tonight and never come back for twenty years, she'd still be waiting for me!"

"My dear fellow!"

"Well?"

"If you actually failed to keep your appointment with her?"

"Actually that."

"Well," said Gerald carelessly, "putting all due respect to your lady to the side so that we may speak freely..."

"Go ahead," said Tommy Vance.

"Well, then, speaking on the basis of what I've seen and heard, I'd venture that if you go away tonight and don't come back for ten days—"

"Well?" exclaimed Tommy.

"When you came back, you'd find a cold reception, Tommy."

"I could explain everything in five seconds."

"Suppose she'd grown lonely in the meantime? If she's a pretty girl and the town's full of young fellows with nothing to do in the evening... you understand, Vance."

There was a groan from Vance as the iron of doubt entered his spirit.

"It makes me sort of sick," he murmured. "How do I know what she'd do? But no, she'd never look at another gent!"

"How long have you been engaged?" asked Gerald.

"Oh, about a month."

"Have you been away from her for more than twelve hours during that time?"

"No," admitted Tommy reluctantly.

"My dear fellow, then you know that you're talking simply from guesswork."

Tommy was quiet, breathing hard. At length he said: "If she was to draw away from me simply because I missed seeing her one night and was away for ten days, why, I'd never speak to her again. I'd never want to see her again!"

But Gerald laughed.

"That's what they usually say," he declared. "But after the smoke has cleared away, they settle back to happiness again. They wear a scar, but they try to forget. They wish themselves back into a blind state. And so they marry. Ten years later they begin to remember. They hearken back to the old wounds, and then comes the crash! That's what wrecks a home..."

He broke off and changed his tone before he went on: "But of course no man dares to test a woman before he makes her his wife. He tests a horse before he buys it; he tests gold before he mines for it; but he doesn't get a proof in the most important question of all! Pure blindness, Tom Vance!"

"Suppose...," groaned Tommy Vance, his head lowered.

He did not finish his sentence. He did not need to, for Gerald could tell the wretched suspicion which was beginning to grow in his companion.

"But you see there's never a chance for it," said Gerald. "There's a small, prophetic voice in a man which tells him that he dare not make the try. He knows well enough that, if the girl is ready to marry, she'll marry someone else, if she doesn't marry him. It's the home-making instinct in her that's forcing her ahead. That's all as clear as daylight, I think."

"Good Lord!" groaned Tommy. "Suppose I should be wrong!"

"Come, come," said Gerald. "I didn't mean that you should take me seriously. I was merely talking about girls in general."

"I wish I'd never heard you speak," said Tommy bitterly.

"You'll forget what I've said by tomorrow... by the time she's smiled at you twice," said Gerald.

"Not if I live a hundred years," said Tommy. "And why not do it? As you say we test gold before we dig for it... and only ten days!"

He rubbed his hand across his forehead.

"You won't do it," said Gerald. "When it comes to the pinch, you won't be able to get away."

"What makes you so sure?" asked Tommy in anger.

He was boy enough to be furious at the thought that any one could see through him.

"Why, as I said before," went on Gerald, fighting hard to retain his calmness and keep his voice from showing unmistakable signs of his excitement, "as I said before, there's something inside of you which keeps whispering that I'm right!"

"By the Lord," groaned Tommy, "I won't admit it."

"No, like the rest you'll close your eyes to it."

"But if at the end of ten days..."

"That's the point. If at the end of ten days, you came back and found her dancing with another man, smiling for him, laughing for him, working hard to make him happy, why..."

"I'd kill him!" breathed Tommy Vance.

"Of course you would," said Gerald. "And that's another reason you must not go away. It might lead to a manslaughter."

Tommy tore open his shirt at the throat as though he were strangling, and yet the wind was humming down the valley, and the night air was chill and piercing. It was late November, and winter was already on the upper mountains, covering them with white hoods.

"You're so cussed sure!" said Tommy Vance.

"Of course."

"What gives you the right to talk so free and easy?"

"I'd wager a thousand dollars on it," said Gerald.

"The devil you would!"

"I'm not asking you to take up the bet," tempted Gerald.

"I could cover that amount."

"But a thousand dollars and a girl is a good deal to put up."

"Kern, I'll make the bet!"

"Have you lost your wits, Tom Vance?"

It was too wonderfully good to be true, but now he must drive the young fellow so far that he could not draw back.

"I mean every word of it," Tom said.

"I don't believe it! Think of what will go on in the girl's head, Tom. She's waiting for you now. She'd worry a good deal if she didn't hear from you till the morning and then got only a little bit of a note:

Dear Kate:
Have to be away on business. No time to explain. Back in ten days.
Tom

"A note like that, my boy, would make her wild with anger. A girl doesn't like to be treated lightly."

"But I," said Tommy Vance, "am going to send her just such a note."

"Tush! That's mere bravado even from you."

"Kern, is my word good for my money?"

"Good as gold."

"Then I'm gone tonight, and when I come back in ten days if she's... she's as much as cold to me, you win one thousand dollars!"

He turned away. Gerald caught him by the shoulder.

"Tom," he said, "I'm not going to let you do this. I'd feel the burden of the responsibility. And mind you, my friend, if the girl is not as strong as you think she is, and as constant, it is simply the working of Mother Nature in her. Will you try to see that?"

"I've come to my conclusion, Kern, let me go!"

"It's final?"

"Absolutely!"

"Ten whole days?"

"Ten whole days!"

"With never a word to her during all that time?"

"With never a word to her during all that time!"

The hand of Gerald dropped away. He stepped back with an almost solemn feeling of wonder passing over that crafty brain of his. How mysterious was the power of words which could enter the brain and so pervert the good sense of a man as the sense of Tommy Vance had been changed by his subtle suggestions!

"Well," said he when he could control his voice, "you're a brave fellow, Tom Vance!"

"Good night!" snapped Tommy over his shoulder.

"And good luck!" sang out Gerald.

He watched his late companion melt into the shadows, and then Gerald turned to saunter on his way. It was all like the working of a miracle. Without the lifting of his hand he had driven from Culver City the only man who stood between him and a pleasant visit with lovely Kate Maddern.

No matter if she were already engaged to another man. One curt note, and then ten days of silence could do much. Oh, it could do very much. Wounded pride was an excellent sedative for the most vital pangs of love. And silence and the leaden passing of time would help. Ten days to a lover were the ten eternities of another person.

Would it be very odd if she came to pay some attention to a stranger who was not altogether ungracious, whose manners were easy, whose voice was gentle, who could tell her many tales of many lands, and the story of whose manhood was even now ringing through Culver Valley—if such a man as this were near while Kate Maddern struggled with grief and pride and angry pique, would there not be a chance to win a thousand dollars from Tom Vance—and something more?

V. — THE CAMPAIGN BEGINS

He went lazily on up the slope of the mountain. Behind him the town was wakening to a wilder life. And, staring back, he could see a thickening stream which poured in under the great light in front of Canton Douglas's place.

Yes, it would be very pleasant to sit at one of those tables and mine the gold out of the pockets of the men who were there with their wealth. But a game even more exciting was ahead of him. He turned up the hill again, walking lightly and swiftly now. Yonder was the cabin, with the door open and a spurt of yellow lamplight over the threshold and dripping down half a dozen stone steps.

He arrived at the path and turned up it, and in a moment she came whipping through the door and down the steps with a cloak flying behind her shoulders.

"Tommy, Tommy dear!" she was calling as she came dancing to him. Her arms flashed around his neck. She had kissed him twice before she realized her mistake. And then horror made her too numb to flee. She merely gasped and shrank away from him.

"I beg your pardon," said Gerald. "This is the second time I've been mistaken for Tommy dear.' Do I look so much like him in the darkness?"

"What have I done!" breathed poor Kate.

She went up the steps backward, keeping her face to him as though she feared that he would spring in pursuit the moment she turned her back. But at the top step, near the door of the cabin, she paused.

"Who are you?" she queried from this post of vantage.

"My name is Gerald Kern," he said.

"Have you come to see Dad?"

"No."

"Are you one of the men from the next cabin?"

"No."

"Well?" inquired Kate tentatively.

"I came to see you," said Gerald.

"You came to see me? I don't remember..."

"Ever meeting me?"

"Have I?"

"Never! So here I am, if you don't mind."

She hesitated. It was plain that she. was interested. It was also plain that she was a little alarmed.

"I came down the hill this afternoon," he went on. "Rather, it was in the dark of the twilight, and some one called from the door of the cabin to 'Tommy dear.'"

"I'm so ashamed!" said Kate Maddern.

"You needn't be. It was very pleasant. It brought me back up this mortal hill in the hope that you might let me talk to you for five minutes. To you and your father, you know."

"Oh, to me and to Dad."

There was a hint of laughter in her voice which told him that she understood well enough.

"I didn't know anyone who'd introduce me, you see."

"I think you manage very nicely all by yourself," said Kate Maddern.

"Thank you."

"You are just new to Culver City?"

"Yes. All new this evening."

"But you haven't come to dig gold... in such clothes as those."

"I'm only looking at the country, you know."

"And you don't know a single man here?"

"Only one I met at Canton Douglas's place."

"That terrible place! Who was it?"

"His name was Vance."

"Why, that's Tommy!"

"Your Tommy?"

"Of course!"

"Lord bless us!" said Gerald. "If I had known that it was he, I should never have let him go."

"Go where?"

"He's off to find a mine... or prospect a new ledge, I think."

"He left tonight?"

There was bewilderment and grief in her voice.

"Yes. I'm so sorry that I bring bad news. Shall I go back to find him?"

"Will you?"

"Of course. If I had guessed that he was your Tommy, I should have tried to dissuade him."

He turned away.

"Come back!" she called.

He faced her again.

"Don't go another step! I... I mustn't pursue him, you know."

"Just as you wish," he answered.

"But what a strange thing for Tommy Vance to do!"

"Wasn't it?"

"And to start prospecting in the middle of night..."

"Very odd, of course. But all prospectors are apt to do queer things, aren't they?"

"Without saying a word to me about it!" And she stamped her foot.

"Hello?" called a voice beyond the cabin, and then a man turned the corner of the shack.

"Dad!"

"Well, honey?"

"What do you think of Tommy?"

"The same as ever. What do you think?"

"I think he's queer... very queer!"

"Trouble with him?"

"Dad, he was to come to see me tonight. It was extra specially important."

"And he didn't come?"

"He left town!"

"Terrible!" murmured her father and laughed.

"Dad, he's gone prospecting. Without a word to me."

"Leave Tom alone. He's a good boy. Hello, there!"

He had come gradually forward, and now he caught sight of Gerald, a dim form among the shadows.

"That's the man who has just told me about Tom."

"H'm!" growled Maddern. "Did Tommy ask you to bring us the news?" he asked of Gerald.

"No, Mr. Maddern."

"You know me, do you?"

"I know your name."

"Well, sir, you might have let Tom talk for himself."

"It was quite by accident that I told your daughter," he said.

"I don't believe it," said Maddern. "A pretty girl hears more bad news about young men from other young men than an editor of a paper. Oh, I was young, and I know how it goes. It was by accident you told her, eh?"

"Dad, you mustn't talk like that!"

"You don't need to steer me, honey. I'll talk my own way along. I've got along unhelped for fifty years. It was accident, eh?"

"It was," said Gerald.

"And that's a lie, young man."

"You are fifty, are you not?"

"And what of it?"

"You are old enough to know better than to talk to a stranger as you talk to me."

Maddern came swooping down the steps. There was no shadow of doubt that he was of a fighting stock and full of blood royal which hungered for battle.

"Dad!" cried the girl from above.

"Don't be alarmed," said Gerald. "Nothing will happen."

"What makes you so infernally sure of that?"

"A still small voice is speaking to me from inside," said Gerald.

And suddenly rage mastered him. It was the one defect in his nature that from time to time these overmastering impulses of fury would sweep across him. He lowered his voice to a whisper which could not reach the girl, but what he said to Maddern was: "You overbearing fool, step down the hill with me away from the girl, and I'll tell you some more about yourself."

To his amazement, Maddern chuckled.

"This lad has spirit," he said cheerfully. "Ain't you going to introduce me, Kate?"

"This is my father?" said Kate.

"I have gathered that," said Gerald.

"And, Dad, this is Gerald Kern, who was just..."

"Gerald Kern?" shouted Maddern, leaping back a full yard. "Are you the one that... come up here!"

He caught Gerald by the arm and literally dragged him up the stairs and into the shaft of light which streamed through the open door.

"It's him!" he thundered to the girl as he stood back from Gerald, a rosy-cheeked, white-haired man with an eye as bright as a blue lake among mountains of snow. "It's the one that kicked Red Charlie out of town. Oh, lad, that was a good job. Another day, and I'd've got myself killed trying to fight the hound. When he talked to me, it was like a spur digging me in the ribs. But Charlie's gone, and you're the man that started him running! Gimme your hand!" And he wrung the fingers of Gerald Kern with all his force.

This was pleasant enough, but in the background what was the girl doing? She was regarding the stranger with wonder which went from his odd riding boots to his riding trousers, thence up to his face. But anon her glance wandered toward the trail outside the house again, and the heart of Gerald sank. Truly, she was even more deeply smitten than he had dreaded to find her.

But William Maddern was taking him into his house and heart like a veritable lost brother.

"Come inside and sit down, man," went on Maddern. "Sit down and let me hear you talk. By Heaven, it did me good to hear the story. I'd liave given a month of life to see Red Charlie when the lanterns and the other truck landed on him. Kate, you can stand watch for Tommy."

Gerald was dragged inside the house.

"Why should I watch?" said Kate.

"Make yourself busy," said Maddern. "We're going to have a talk."

"Am I too young to hear man-talk?" asked Kate angrily, standing at the door.

"Now there's the woman of it," said her father with a grin. "Lock a door, and she's sure to break her heart unless she can open it, even if she has all the rest of the house to play in. But if you're inside, you'll be sure to wish you were out to wait for Tommy Vance."

She tossed her head.

"Let him stay away," she said. "But not to have sent a single word, Dad!"

And Gerald bit his lip to keep from smiling. It was all working out as though charmed.

"When I was a youngster in Montana," began Maddern, "I remember a fellow in the logging camp as like Red Charlie as two peas in a pod. And when..."

With one tenth of his mind, Gerald listened. With all the rest he dwelt on Kate. And she was all that he had hoped. The glimpse had been a true promise. Now for a season of careful diplomacy and unending effort. Were not ten days long enough for a great campaign?

VI. — GERALD MEETS CHEYENNE CURLY

But ten days were not enough! Not a day that he left unimproved. Not a day that he did not manage to see Kate Maddern. But still all was not as it should be. He felt the shadowy thought of big, handsome Tom Vance ever in her mind. It fell between them in every silence during their conversation.

Not that he himself was unwelcome, for she liked him at once and showed her liking with the most unaffected directness. But sometimes he felt that friendship is farther from love than the bitterest hate, even.

In the meantime, he had become a great man in Culver City. The sinews of war he provided by a short session every evening in Canton Douglas's place—a very short session, for it must never come to the ear of the girl that he was a professional gambler who drew his living from the cards. To her, and to the rest of Culver City, he was the ideal of the careless gentleman, rich, idle, with nothing to do except spend every day more happily than the days before it.

Neither was there any need for more battle to establish his prowess. It was taken for granted on all hands that he was invincible. Men made way for him. They turned to him with deference. He was considered as one apart from the ordinary follies of lesser men. He was an umpire in case of dispute; he was a final authority. And the sheriff freely admitted that this stranger had lessened his labors by half. For quarrels and gun play did not flourish under the regime of Gerald Kern.

There was the case of Cheyenne Curly, for instance. Cheyenne had built him a repute which had endured upon a solid foundation for ten years. He was not one of these showy braggarts. He was a man who loved battle for its own sake. He had fought here and there and everywhere. If he could not lure men into an engagement with guns, he was willing to fall back upon knife play, in which he was an expert after the Mexican school; and if knives were too strong for the stomach of his companion, he would agree to a set-to with bare fists. Such was Cheyenne Curly. Men avoided him as they avoided a plague.

And in due time, stories of the strange dandy who was "running" Culver City drifted across the hills and came to the ear of the formidable Curly. It made him prick his ears like a grizzly scenting a worthy rival.

Before dawn he had made his pack and was on the trail of the new battle.

None who saw it could forget the evening on which Cheyenne arrived in Culver City. He strode into Canton Douglas's place and held forth at the bar, bracing his back against a corner of the wall. There he waited until the enemy should arrive.

Canton Douglas himself left his establishment and went to give Gerald warning. He found that hero reading quietly in his room, reading the Bible and...

But that story should be told in the words of Canton himself.

"I come up the hall wheezing and panting, and I bang on Gerald's door," he narrated. "Gerald sings out for me to come in. I jerk open the door, and there he sits done up as usual like he was just out of a bandbox.

"'Hello,' says he, standing up and putting down the big book he was reading. 'I'm very glad to see you, Mr. Douglas. Sit down with me.'

"'Mr. Kern,' says I, 'there's hell popping.'

"'Let it pop,' says he. 'I love noise of kinds.'

"'Cheyenne Curly's here looking for you,' says I.

"'Indeed?' says he. 'I don't remember the gentleman?'

"I leaned ag'in the wall.

"'He's a nacheral-born hell-cat,' says I. 'He don't live on nothing less'n fire. He's clawed up more gents than would fill this room. He'd walk ten miles and swim a river for the sake of a fight.'

"'And he has come here hunting trouble with me?' says Gerald.

"'He sure has,' says I.

"'But I'm a peaceable man and an upholder of the law, am I not?', says Gerald.

"'Which you sure are, Mr. Kern,' says I. 'When you play in my house, I know that there ain't going to be no gun fights or no loud talk. And that's the straight of it, too.'

"'Very well,' says he. 'Then, if you won't stay with me and try a few of these walnuts and some of this excellent home-made wine... if you insist on going back immediately... you may tell Mr. Cheyenne Curly that I am most pacifically disposed, and that I am more interested in my book than in the thought of his company.'

"I let the words come through my head slow and sure. Didn't seem like I could really be hearing the man that had cleaned up Red Charlie. I backed up to the door, and then I got a sight of the book that he was reading. And... by the Lord, boys, it was the Bible! Wow! It near dropped me. I was slugged that hard by the sight of that book! Yep, it was an honest Injun Bible all roughed up along the edges with the gilt half tore off, it had been carried around so much and used so much.

"Well, sir, it didn't fit in with Gerald the way we knew him, so quick with a gun and so handy with a pack of cards. But, after all, it did fit in with him, because he always looked as cool and as easy as a preacher even when he was in a fight. It give me another look into the insides of him, and everything that I seen plumb puzzled me. Here he was reading a Bible, and the rest of us down yonder wondering whether he'd be alive five seconds after he'd met Cheyenne Curly! He seen me hanging there in the doorway, and he started to make talk with me. Always free and easy, Gerald is. He sure tries to make a gent comfortable all the time.

"He says to me: 'I get a good deal of enjoyment out of this old book. Do you read it much, Mr. Douglas?'

"'Mr. Kern,' says I, 'I ain't much of a hand with religion. I try to treat every man as square as I can and as square as he treats me. That's about as much religion as I got time for.'

"'Religion?' says he. 'Why, man, the Bible is simply a wonderful story book.'

"Yes, sir, them was his words. And think of a man that could read the Bible because of the stories in it! Speaking personal, there's too many 'ands' in it. They always stop me!

"'Well,' says I to Gerald, 'I'll go down and tell Cheyenne that you're too busy to see him tonight. He'll have to call later.'

"'Exactly,' says he. 'One can't be at the beck and call of every haphazard stranger, Mr. Douglas.'

"'No, sir,' says I. 'But the trouble with Cheyenne is that he ain't got no politeness, and that when I tell him that, he's mighty liable to come a-tearing up here and knock down your door to get at you.'

"At that, Gerald lays down his book and shuts it over his finger to keep the place. He looks at me with a funny twinkle in his eye.

"'Dear, dear,' says he, 'is this Cheyenne such a bad man as all that? Would he actually break down my door?'

"'He would,' says I, 'and think nothing of it.'

"'In that case,' says he, 'you might tell him that I am reading the story of Saul, and that when I have finished I may feel inclined to take the air. I may even come into your place, Mr. Douglas. Will you be good enough to tell him that?'

"'Mr. Kern,' says I, 'I sure wish you luck. And if he gets you, there ain't a chance for him to get out of this town alive.'

"At that he jumps up, mad as can be.

"'Sir,' says he, 'I hope I have misunderstood you. If there should be an altercation between me and another man, I know that the victor would never be touched by the mob.'

"'All right,' says I and backed out the door feeling as though I'd stepped into a hornet's nest.

"I come downstairs and back to my place. There's Cheyenne Curly still standing at the bar with his back to the wall. He ain't drinking none. And all the half of the bar next to him is empty. The boys are doing their drinking in front of the other half. And Curly is waiting and waiting and not saying nothing to nobody, but his shiny little pig eyes are clamped on the door all the time.

"I go up to him and say: 'Curly, Gerald is plumb busy reading a book, but when he gets through with it he says that he's coming down to have a little talk to you.'

"Curly don't say nothing back. He just runs the tip of his tongue over the edge of his beard and grins to himself like I'd just promised him a Christmas dinner. Made my blood turn cold to look at him.

"Then we started in waiting... me and every other man in my place, and there was a clear path from the door to the place where Curly was standing at the bar. But outside that path nobody was afraid of getting hurt. When two like Gerald and Curly started the bullets flying, every slug would go where it was aimed.

"It wasn't more'n half an hour, but it seemed like half a year to all of us, before the swinging doors come open and in walks Gerald. He was done up extra special that night. He had a white silk handkerchief wrapped around his throat like he was afraid of the cold. His boots shined like two lanterns. And the gun he was carrying wasn't no place to be seen. Matter of fact, just where he aims to pack his gun we ain't been able to make out... he gets it out so slick and easy out of nowhere.

"I looked over to Curly. And there he was crouched a little and with his right hand glued to the butt of his gun, and he was trembling all over, he was so tensed up for a lightning-quick draw.

"But his hand hung on the gun. He didn't draw, and I wondered why.

"I looked down to Gerald. And by Heaven, sir, he wasn't facing Curly at all. He'd turned to one side and he was talking to young Hank Meyers. Yes, sir, with that wild cat all ready to jump at his throat, Gerald had turned his back on him, pretty near, and he was standing over by the table of Hank.

"Everything was as silent as the inside of a morgue. You could hear every word Gerald was saying. And his voice was like silk, it was so plumb easy.

"'I haven't seen you since the last mail, Mr. Meyers,' he was saying. 'What is the word from your sick mother now?'

"Well, sir, hearing him talk like that sent a shiver through me. It wasn't nacheral or human, somehow, for a gent to be as calm and cool as that.

"Hank tried to talk back, but all he could do was work his lips. Finally, he managed to say that the last mail brought him a letter saying that his mother was a lot better. And Gerald drops a hand on Hank's shoulder.

"'I'm very glad to hear the good news,' he says. 'I congratulate you on receiving it. I have a little engagement here, and when I'm through I'll come back to you and hear some more, if I may.'

"You could hear every word clear as a bell. He turns back again.

"Curly was still crouched, and now he yanks his gun half clear of the holster, but Gerald leans over and takes out a handkerchief and flicks it across the toe of his boot.

"'Beastly lot of dust in the street,' he says.

"Well, sir, there was a sort of a groan in the room. We was all keyed up so high it was like a violin string breaking in the middle of a piece. I was shaking like a scared kid.

"But finally Gerald straightened and come right up toward Curly. I looked at Curly, expecting to see his gun jump. But there was nary a gun in his hand. Maybe he was waiting for Gerald to make the first move, I thought. And then I seen that Curly's eyes were glassy. His mouth was open, and his jaw was beginning to sag. And he was shaking from head to foot.

"I knew what had happened; that long waiting had busted his nerve wide open the same as it had busted the nerve of the rest of us.

"Up come Gerald straight to him.

"'I understand,' says Gerald, 'that your name is Cheyenne Curly, and that you've come to see me. What is it you wish to say to me, sir?'

"Curly moved his jaw, but didn't say nothing. I could hear the boys breathing hard. Speaking personal, I couldn't breathe at all.

"'I was given to understand further,' says Gerald, 'that you intend to wipe up the ground with me.'

"Curly's hand moved at last. But it swung forward... empty! And I knew that there wasn't going to be no shooting that night. But it was like a nightmare, watching him sort of sag smaller and smaller. Straightened up he must have been about three inches taller'n Gerald. But with Gerald standing there so straight and quiet, he looked like a giant, and Curly looked like a sick boy with a funny beard on his face.

"Hypnotism? I dunno. It was sure queer.

"Pretty soon Curly manages to speak.

"'I was just riding this way,' says Curly, his voice shaking. 'I ain't meaning any harm to you, Mr.

Kern. No harm in the world to you, sir.'

"He starts forward. I felt sick inside. It ain't very pretty to see a brave man turned into a yaller dog like that. Half way to the door Curly throws a look over his shoulder, and then he starts running like he'd seen a gun pointed at him. He went out through the door like a shot. And that was the end of Curly.

"But, speaking personal, you and me, I'd rather hook up with a pair of tornadoes than have to face Gerald with a gun!"

VII. — KATE ROLLS A BOULDER

There were other tales of that famous encounter between Gerald and Cheyenne Curly, that bloodless and horrible battle of nerve against nerve. And certainly the sequel was true, which related how terrible Curly sank low and lower until finally he became cook for a gang of laborers on the road, a despised cook who was kicked about by the feeblest Chinaman in the camp.

There was another aftermath. From that time on, men shunned an encounter with Gerald as though he carried a lightning flash in his eye. For who could tell, no matter how long his record of heroism, what would happen if he should encounter Gerald Kern in Culver City? Who could tell by what wizardry he accomplished his work of unnerving an antagonist? And was it not possible, as Canton Douglas had so often suggested, that there was a species of hypnotism about his way of looking a man squarely in the eye?

Even Kate Maddern was inclined to believe. And Kate was, of all people, the least likely to be drawn by blind enthusiasms. But she talked seriously to Gerald about it the next day.

It was a fortnight since Tommy Vance had disappeared, and Gerald himself was beginning to wonder at the absence of Tom. Was it possible that the young miner had determined to double the test to which he was subjecting himself? December was wearing away swiftly, and still he did not come. It troubled Gerald. It was incomprehensible to him, for he had not dreamed that there was so much metal in his rival. But perhaps it could be explained away as the result of some disaster of trail or camp which had overwhelmed Tommy Vance.

In fact, he became surer and surer as the days went by that Tom would never return—that somewhere among those hard-sided mountains lay his strong young body, perhaps buried deep beneath a snow slide or the thousand tons of an avalanche.

And yet there was no feeling of remorse in Gerald, even though it was he whose cunning suggestion had thrust Tom out of the camp. His creed was a simple one: "Get what you can from the world before the world gets what it can from you."

In his own life he had never encountered mercy, and for mercy he did not look in his dealings with others. He gave no quarter, because he expected none. And if, from time to time, the honest and happy face of Tom Vance rose before him, Tom Vance with his eyes shining with the thought of Kate—if that thought rose for a moment, it was quickly forgotten again. Did not an old maxim say that all was fair in love or in war?

And he loved Kate profoundly, beyond belief. He could no longer be alone. The thought of her followed him. It fell like a shadow across the page of the book he was reading. It whispered and stirred behind his chair. It laid a phantom hand upon his shoulder and breathed upon him in the wind.

Yet for all the vividness with which he kept the thought of her near him, she was always new. And on this bleak morning, as December grew old, it seemed to Gerald that it was a new girl who welcomed him at the door of her cabin.

He studied her curiously. All these days he had been waiting and waiting. There was something in her which kept certain words he was hungry to say locked behind his teeth. But this morning, with a bounding heart, he knew that there was a change.

He told her so in so many words.

"Something has happened," he said. "There's been some good news since I saw you yesterday. What is it, Kate?"

"Didn't you see when you came up the steps?"

"Nothing," he said thoughtfully. "I saw nothing changed."

She brought him to the door again and threw it open. The strong wind, sharp with cold from the snows, struck them in the face and tugged her dress taut about her body.

"Don't you remember the boulder which used to be beside the door?" she inquired.

"I remember now," he said, looking down to the ragged hollow near the threshold, where the great stone had once lain.

"Now look down the hillside. Do you see that big wet brown stone among all the black ones?"

A hundred yards away, across the road and down the farther slope, he saw the stone she pointed out.

"I pried the boulder up this morning," she said. "All last night I lay awake thinking about it, but finally I made up my mind. This morning I pried it out of its bed, and it rolled down the mountain. It sprang across the road in one bound, and then it fell with a crashing and smashing away off yonder."

She closed the door. They turned back into the room, and Gerald sat down with her near the fire.

"Well," she cried at last, "aren't you going to ask me what it all means?"

"I'd very much like to know," said Gerald.

"You're always the same," said Kate Maddern gloomily. "You keep behind a fence. You're like a garden behind a wall. One never knows what is going on inside. And it isn't fair, Gerald! It's like reading a book that has the last chapter torn out. One never has the ending of the yarn."

He smiled at her anger and said nothing.

"Well, the stone was in the way when we built the shack," she went on at last, still a little sulky. "Dad is very strong, and yet he couldn't budge it. He was about to blast it when Tom Vance came up from the mine. He laid hold of the stone... he's a perfect Hercules, you know... and he tugged until his shoulders creaked. He stirred it, but he couldn't lift it.

"'It's no good,'" Father said. 'You can't budge the stone, Tommy. Don't make a fool of yourself and break your back for nothing.'

"Tommy simply looked at him and at me. Then he jumped back, caught up the stone, and staggered away with it. He dropped it yonder, and when we built the house the stone was by the door."

She paused. Gerald had leaned forward, and she said the rest looking down to the floor.

"I've never been able to see that boulder," she said, "without thinking of Tommy. It meant as much to me as the sound of his voice, and it was just as clear. Can you understand what I mean?"

"Of course," said Gerald sadly. "Of course I can understand."

"But finally," she went on, "I made up my mind last night. Tommy was not coming back. Perhaps he had found some other girl. Perhaps he was tired of me, and he hadn't the words or the courage to tell me about it. So he simply faded away. And this morning I got up and pried out the stone and watched it roll away."

He could raise his eyes no higher than her throat, and there he saw the neck band of her blouse quiver ever so faintly with the hard beating of her heart.

"And after the boulder rolled away," said Gerald at last, "what did you do then?"

"What do you think I did?"

He looked up to her face. She was flushed with a strange excitement.

"You came back and lay on your bed and cried," said Gerald.

"Yes," she whispered. "I did."

"And then..." continued Gerald.

He interrupted himself to draw out a cigarette, and he smoked a quarter of it in perfect silence before he completed his sentence.

"And then," he concluded, "you jumped out and wiped the tears out of your eyes and vowed that you were an idiot for wasting so much time on any man. Is that right?"

"My father saw me, then... and he told you all about it!"

"Not a word."

"But how do you know so well?"

"I make a game of guessing, you see."

She stared at him with a mixture of anger and wonder.

"I wonder," she said, "if there is something about you... something queer... and do you really see into the minds of people?"

"Not a bit," he assured her.

"Do you think I believe that?"

Her head canted a bit to one side, and she smiled at him so wistfully that his heart ached.

"Now that the boulder is gone, Kate, won't you be lonely?"

"On account of a stone? Of course not. And then I have you, Gerald, to keep the blues away, except when you fall into one of your terrible, terrible, endless silences. I almost hate you then."

"Why?"

"Because, when a man is silent too long, it makes a girl begin to feel that he knows all about her."

"And that would be dreadful?"

"Dreadful!" said Kate Maddern and laughed joyously. As though she invited the catastrophe!

"But I'm only a stuffed figure, I'm afraid," said Gerald. "You're like a little girl playing a game. You call me Gerald to my face, but you call me Tommy to yourself, and when you are talking to me you are thinking of him."

She flushed to the eyes.

"What a terrible thing to say!" cried Kate.

"Then it is true?"

"Not a word."

"Ah, Kate," said he, "I guessed it before, but that doesn't lessen the sting of knowing that my guess was right."

She sprang out of the chair.

"Do you imagine that I'm still dreaming about him?" she challenged him.

"I know you are."

"You're wrong. I won't be treated so lightly by any man!" She added: "Besides, I think I always cared for him more as a brother than a sweetheart. We were raised together, you know."

"Ah, yes," said Gerald.

"You're not believing me again?"

"I haven't said that."

"It's gospel truth! And I'll never care for him again. I really never want to see him again. I'm only furious when I think of all the sleep I've lost about his going away!"

How easy, now, to say the adroit and proper words. She had opened the way for him. That was plain. She had thrust the thought of Tom Vance away from her, and she wanted Gerald to fill the vacant room. And yet there was an imp of the perverse in him. He fought against its promptings, but he could not fight hard enough.

He found himself studying her shrewdly. Would it not be delightful to show her how truly weak she was—and make her in another moment weep at the very thought of Tom Vance? He spoke against his more sane, inner promptings.

VIII. — GERALD'S BLINDNESS

"I'm going to tell you a true story," he said. "It will change your mind about Tommy, and it will make you hate me, among other things."

"Do you want me to do that?"

"I can't help telling you," said Gerald. "The devil seems to be in me this morning, making me undo all my hard work. But let's go back to that first evening when I passed you on the hillside."

"Of course I remember."

"I never told you why I came back. But naturally you guessed."

"Naturally," she said. "There aren't many girls in Culver City."

He raised his thin-fingered hand and brushed that thought away. He waved it into nothingness.

"I heard you call," he said, "and then I had a shadowy glimpse of your face in the lamplight. That was enough to catch me. Mind you, it doesn't take much... just the right touch, the right stir of the voice, a glimmer of the eyes, and a man is gone forever. I was riding on a bus in London once. A girl crossed the street and looked up to me with a smile. Not that she was smiling for me, you understand... but there was an inner joyousness..."

He paused to recall it. And Kate Maddern was still as a mouse, listening, her fingers interlaced.

"She was very beautiful," said Gerald. "And if there had been something more, I think I should have climbed off that bus and followed her. But something was lacking."

"A second look, perhaps," suggested the pagan heart of Kate.

He smiled at her.

"You miss my point," he said. "What I am trying to say is that men are sometimes carried away by shams. They think they have found the true thing, and they wake up to learn that their hands are full of fools' gold. But when the reality comes, it has an electric touch. And when I saw you and heard your voice, Kate, I knew that you were the end of the trail."

"Gerald," she said, "you are making love to me shamelessly."

"I am," said he and lighted another cigarette. "But to continue my story... unless it bores you?"

"I am fascinated! Of course I am!"

"Very well. That night I went into Canton Douglas's place, and almost at once I heard some one speak to Tommy. Of course I looked, and the moment I laid eyes on him I knew that this was the man you had called to. He was handsome, clean-eyed, young, strong. He was everything that a man should be. And I managed it so that I should be asked to sit in at their game. I wanted to know more of Tommy Vance. I wanted to test the metal of my enemy."

"Enemy?"

"Because I knew that one of us had to win, and the other one had to lose."

She sat stiff and straight and watched him out of hostile eyes. Whatever kindliness she might feel for him now, might she not lose it if she learned the rest of his story? And yet he kept on. That imp of the perverse was still driving him as it had driven him, on a day, to lead his army of brown-skinned revolutionists into the jaws of death, tempting chance for the very sake of the long odds themselves.

"I watched Tommy Vance like a hawk," he went on. "I was hunting for weaknesses. I was hunting for something which would prove him to be unworthy of you. And if I had found it,"—here he raised his head and met her startled glance squarely—"I should have brushed him from my path with no more care than I feel when my heel crushes a beetle. But as the game went on I saw that he was a fine fellow to the core, brave, generous, kind, and true as steel!"

He wrung those words of commendation from himself one by one.

"And I saw," he went on, "that as long as he was on the ground my case was hopeless."

He paused again.

"Well, in love and in war, Kate, men do bad things. I managed it so that I could leave the game when he did. He was walking up the hill to meet you, and I set myself to prevent him from coming to your cabin. I told myself that if I succeeded there was still a fighting chance for me. But if I failed I would pack up and leave town and forget you if I could, or at least try to obscure the memory of you with other faces and other countries. But luck helped me. There is a jealous string in every lover. I plucked at that until I had Tommy in agony."

"How horrible!" breathed Kate Maddern.

"Yes, wasn't it? But I was fighting for something better than life, and I took every weapon I could lay my hands on! He was a wide-eyed young optimist. But I planted the seed of eternal doubt in him. He began with an unquestioning faith in you. And before half an hour had passed, I had made a wager of a thousand dollars with him that if he left Culver City for a while and let you wonder why he had gone, when he returned he would find that you had forgotten him. Well, he made the wager, and he left the town that same night. And that's where he is now!"

"Oh, poor Tommy!" she cried. "And I've doubted him and hated him all these days, when all the time..."

"When all the time he was simply making the test. But he was right, after all, and I was hopelessly wrong. At least, Kate, I've made a good hard fight out of it. And the other day when I taught you how to manage Sorrow... just for an instant when you leaned and laughed down to me I thought my dream was to come true after all."

He rose from his chair and confronted her courteously.

"But to send him away by trickery... and all these days to let me think... oh, it was detestable!"

"It was detestable," he admitted gravely.

And, encountered by that calm confession, her fire of anger was smothered before it had gained headway. She began to regard him with a sort of blank fear.

"What is it that you do to people?" she asked suddenly, throwing out her hands in a gesture of helplessness. "There is Red Charlie, who stood as though his hands were chained while you shamed him. And there is poor Tommy, of whom you made a fool and sent away. And then there is Cheyenne Curly, whom you have turned from a brave man into a coward! Is it hypnotism?"

"Do you think it is?" he asked. "At least, they have seen the last of me around here."

He tossed his cigarette into the fireplace.

"Perhaps the devil inspires me to mischief, but the good angel who guards you, Kate, forced me to confess, and so all the evil I have done to Tommy is undone again. I'll leave tonight and trail him until I find him. I'll give him back to you as I found him. And, having been tried by fire, you'll go on loving each other to the end of time!"

He picked up his hat.

"You see that I retain one grace in a graceless life. I shall not ask you to forgive me, Kate."

"You are going... really?"

"Yes."

"To get Tommy?"

"Yes."

"For Heaven's sake, Gerald, don't do that!"

The hat dropped from his finger tips.

"What on earth do you mean?"

"I mean... nothing! Only, don't you see...?"

She had fallen deeper and deeper into a confusion of words from which she could not extricate herself. Now she looked around her as though searching for a place of retreat.

"Won't you understand?" she pleaded.

"Understand what?" asked Gerald huskily.

Then, as some wild glimmer of hope dawned on his brain, he sprang to her and drew her to the window so that the gray and pale light of the winter day beat remorselessly into her face.

"Kate!" he cried. "Speak to me!"

She had buried her face in the crook of her arm.

"Let me go!" whispered Kate.

Instantly, his hands fell away from her. And there she stood blindly swaying.

"Oh," she said, "it is hypnotism. And what have you done to me? What have you done to me?"

"I've loved you, my dear, with all the strength that is in me!"

"Hush!"

"It is solemn truth."

She broke into inexplicable tears and dropped into a chair, and Gerald, white-faced, trembling as Cheyenne Curly had trembled in Canton's place, stood beside her.

"Tell me what I can do, Kate. Anything... and I'll do it. But it tortures me with fire to see you weep!"

"Only don't leave me," she whispered.

He was instantly on his knees beside her.

"I didn't know until you spoke of going," she sobbed. "And then it came over me in a wave. I had never really loved Tommy. He was simply a big brother. I was simply so used to him. You see that, Gerald?"

"I'm trying to see it, dear. But my mind is a blank. I can't make out what is happening, except that you are not hating me as I thought you would, Kate. Is that true?"

"Come closer!"

He leaned nearer her covered face. And suddenly she caught at him and pressed her face into the hollow of his shoulder.

"How can you be so blind!" she breathed. "Oh, don't you see, and haven't you seen almost from the first, that I have loved you, Gerald? And, oh, even when you tell all that is worst in you, it only makes me care for you more and more. What have you done to me?"

"Kismet!" murmured Gerald and, raising his head high, he looked up to the raw-edged rafters and through them and beyond them to the hope of heaven.

IX. — A CHANCE FOR A KINGDOM

An hour later, Gerald was riding Sorrow straight into the heart of a snow-laden wind, for some action he must have to work out the delirious joy which filled him, and which packed and crammed his body to a frenzy of recklessness. The very edge of the wind was nothing to him and, when the driven snow stung his lips, he laughed at it. For this was his home land, his native country, and all that it held was good to him, for was it not the land, also, which held Kate Maddern?

Lord bless her, and again, Lord bless her! He laughed to himself once more, and this time with tears in his eyes, to think how blind he had been to the truth. And he remembered how, with tears and with laughter, she had confessed that the rolling away of the boulder and the telling of that story to him had all been anxiously planned before in the hope that he would speak then, if ever.

"And I shall be good to her," said Gerald solemnly to himself. "I shall be worthy of her. Yes, I shall be very worthy of her, so far as a man may be! I shall make her a queen. I shall give her all the beauty of background which she needs. Her hand on velvet... a jewel at her throat and another in her hair..."

His thoughts darted away, every one winged. The energy which he had wasted here and there and everywhere he would now concentrate upon the grand effect. No matter for the wild failures which had marked his past. Was not even the young manhood of Napoleon filled with vain effort and foolish adventures? There was still time and to spare for the founding of an empire!

It was a glorious ride, and the flush of glory was still in his cheeks and bright in his eyes when he came back to the hotel. And there, in the window, he saw a great, rough wreath of evergreen. He studied it in amazement. It was not like Culver City to waste time and energy on such adornments when there was gold to be dug.

Of the proprietor, behind the stove inside, he asked his question.

"And you don't know?" asked the latter with a twinkle in his eye.

"Of what?" asked Gerald.

"It's Christmas, man! Tomorrow will be Christmas! And tonight will be Christmas Eve!"

Gerald stared at him, then laughed aloud with the joy of it. This surely was the hand of fate, which brought him for a present, on the eve of the day of giving, Kate Maddern and all her beauty and all her heart and soul, like a great empire!

He went up the stairs still laughing, with the voice of the proprietor coming dimly behind him: "There's a gentleman waiting in your room for you, Mr. Kern. He looked like I might tell him to go up and make himself to home..."

The rest was lost and Gerald, kicking open the door of his room, looked across to no other than Louis Jerome Banti sitting in Gerald's chair and pouring over Gerald's own Bible. The act in which he was engaged shocked Gerald hardly less than the sight of Banti's face in this place. It was like seeing the devil busy over the word of God.

"In the name of heaven, Banti," he said, "how do you come here?"

"In the name of despair, Monsieur Lupri, what keeps you here?"

"Hush!" cautioned Gerald, raising his finger. "There are ears in the wall to hear that name."

"Are there not?" and Banti chuckled, rubbing his hands together. "Yes, ears in the stones to hear, and a tongue in the wind to give warning of it!"

They shook hands, and as their fingers touched a score of wild pictures slid through the memory of Gerald, fleeter than the motion picture flashes its impressions on the screen—a cold winter morning on a road in Provence, with the crackle of the exhaust thrown back to them from the hills as their machine fled among the naked vineyards—and a night on the Bosphorus when they were stealing, with their launch full of desperadoes, toward the great hulk of the Turkish man-of-war—and a day in hot Smyrna when the...

"Banti here... Banti of all men, and in this of all places."

"And you, my dear Gerald?"

"How did you find me? How on earth did you trail me?"

"How does one follow the path of fire? By the burned things it has touched."

"But I left you with the death sentence..."

"Over my head, and three days of life before me."

"Yes, yes! I had done my best..."

"And it was better than you knew. The poor girl loved you, Gerald. On my soul, I sorrowed for her when I heard her talk. But she it was who came to me at last. With her own hand she opened the doors for me. She guided me to the last threshold. She put a purse fat with gold in my pocket. She pointed out the way to escape, and she gave me the blessing of Allah and this little letter in French for you... for her beloved... her hero of fire and steel."

"Be still, Banti, in the name of heaven!"

He took the little wrinkled envelope. He tore open the end of it. Then, pausing, he lighted a match and touched it to the paper. The flame flared. The letter burned to red-hot ash, fluttered from his finger tips, and reached the floor as a crumbling and wrinkled sheet of gray. A draft caught it and whirled it into nothingness.

"And that is the end?" quietly said Banti, who had watched all this from a little distance. "And yet there was an aroma in the words of that letter, I dare swear, that would have drawn the winged angels lower out of heaven to hear them!"

"It is better this way," said Gerald. "I burn the letter, and I send the fair thoughts back to the fair lady."

"And her fat papa," said Banti.

"And to her fat papa. And now... Banti, you have not changed. You are the same!"

"The very same," said Banti, and drew himself up proudly to the full of his height. He was a glorious figure of a man. And the cunning of his hand was second only to the cunning of his brain. Well did Gerald know it. Had he not, for three long months in Wintry Moscow, dueled with this man a duel in the dark, a thousand shrewd strokes delivered and parried under cover of the darkness of polite intrigue? They had learned to read each other then, and they had learned to dread and respect each other, also. Victory in that battle had fallen to Gerald, but it was a Pyrrhic conquest.

"It is gold, then," said Banti. "It is gold that keeps you here?"

"No."

"A mystery, then?"

Gerald shrugged his shoulders.

"No matter. You will come with me?"

Gerald shook his head.

"No?" and Banti smiled. "But listen... there is a kingdom in the sea!"

"Damn the sea and its kingdoms," said Gerald. "This is my country. And here I stay!"

"There is a kingdom waiting in the sea," said Banti. "Ah, I laugh with the joy of it, monsieur, when I think! Gerald, dear fellow, we are rich men, great men. The task awaits us!"

"Banti, I shall not listen. And it is useless for you to talk."

"In two words, Gerald, what has happened to you?"

"I have a charm against your temptations. I have a flower to defy Circe, Louis."

"A woman?"

"My wife-to-be."

"She shall go with us, then. Where there is a king, may there not be a queen?"

"You are talking to the wind."

"You have not heard me yet."

"I don't wish to."

"You are afraid, then, in spite of your charm?"

"Talk if you must, and the devil take you."

"There is a kingdom in the sea... there is an island in the sea, Monsieur Caprice. Four great powers of Europe and Asia have reached for it... their hands met... and not a finger touched it. So, in mortal fear of one another, they withdrew. They made a compact. They erected the savage chief into a king. They erected the island into a kingdom in the sea, and they swore neutrality. But kings need wars for diversion and, since he could do no better, this amiable idiot of a fat man-eater began to fight with his own subjects. In a trice, a musical comedy set.

"Yonder stands the commerce of the world licking its chops at the sight of the spices of that island and the river dripping with unmined gold and the mountains charged with iron ores and coal, the swamps foul with oil... but yonder is the king fighting his subjects. The island is split into halves. The king holds all the lowlands and the rich towns. The young cousin, with more brains in his little finger than in the whole sconce of the king, holds the uplands with a few hundred stout brigands and makes a living by inroad. Commerce is at a standstill. They kill a white man for the sake of his shoes. And the great, neutral nations and the great, neutral merchants stand about like a circle of lions and find one consolation... that no one is getting a piece of the dainty.

"But now, Gerald, enters a man of brains and money. He sees inspiration. He comes to me. He says: 'I give you money and a shipload of arms and a score of good men. Not too many, or my hand will be too apparent. I send you away. Your ship is wrecked... by unlucky chance... on the shore of the island. You go inland. You open communication with the young prince in the highlands. You offer him money and guns if he will give you the direction of his war. You, with your tact and your diplomacy, make a conquest of that young prince, who is man enough to appreciate a man. He takes you to his heart and into his councils. He turns over his army to you. The guns and the money are brought up. Your few white men are your bodyguard. You train the army of natives for a month. When they can strike the side of a mountain at fifty paces, you invade the domains of the king. In another month, you have routed him. You establish a new regime. You admit my money into your interior. And of the profits which come out of my ventures, one half goes to the kingdom... that is, to you... and the other half goes to me.'

"This, Gerald, is what the man of money and brains says to me. And I reply: 'This is all very well. If I were a Napoleon, I should undertake the task. I should agree to do all these things, ingratiate myself with the colored potentate, become ruler of him and his army, and conquer the kingdom. But I am not Napoleon. I am, however, one of his marshals. In a word, I know the man. Give me only six months to bring him to you!'

"That, Gerald, was my reply, and here I am. Pack up your luggage. Pay your bills... I have ten thousand, and half of it is yours... and come with me at once. We can reach a train by tomorrow morning!"

He stopped, panting with the effort, and he found that Gerald was twining his hands together and then tearing them apart and staring down at the floor. But at last he raised his head.

"No," he said, "I cannot."

"In the name of heaven, Gerald! It is all as I have said! All that is needed to turn the dream into real gold is your matchless hand, your brain!"

"No again. A month ago, I should have gone with you. Today, not if you offered me England and its empire! Banti, you waste words!"

Banti was pale with despair, but he had learned long years before that words are sometimes worse than wasted. He maintained a long silence.

"Gerald," he said at last, "if I may see the lady, my long trip will not have been wasted!"

X. — THE GATHERING OF THE STORM

Footfalls stormed up the stairs, clumped down the hall, and a heavy hand beat on the door.

"Come!" said Gerald as Banti discreetly turned his face to the window.

The door was thrown open by Canton himself.

"Kern," he said, "there's some devilish bad luck! Young Vance..."

He stopped as he caught sight of Banti.

"This is my friend, Mr. George Ormonde," said Gerald. "And this is my friend, Canton Douglas."

Gravely, having received a glance, Banti advanced, bowed, and shook hands.

"You may say anything you wish," said Gerald," before Mr. Ormonde."

"It's Vance come back raving and crazy," said Canton. "He's been out, and he struck it rich... rich as the very devil. He came back, went to see Kate Maddern, and then came down to town like a lion. I dunno what happened between them two. Maybe you know that better than me. But Vance calls you all kinds of names and says that he'll prove 'em on you when he meets you. He's been in my place, saying that he'll come there again at eight tonight, and that he expects to find you there."

"Very well," said Gerald. "I'll meet him."

Was it not better, once and for all, to have the matter ended and poor Tommy Vance out of the way?

"It's got to be that?" said Canton sadly. "But Tommy's white, Kern. Ain't there any other way?"

"There would have been," said Gerald, "if the fool had come in private to me. But now that he's challenged me before the town, can I do anything but meet him?"

"It don't look like there's no way," and Canton sighed. "But it's a mighty big shame."

"It is" said Gerald. "He's a fine fellow. I've no desire to meet him with a gun."

"Suppose he were to be arrested and locked up till he got over this..."

"Do you think he ever will get over it?" asked Gerald.

Canton hung his head.

"It's a mess," he muttered. "I dunno what to think... except that it's the devil."

"Go back and tell the boys that I'll be there," said Gerald, and Canton left the room sadly.

Banti sat down again, whistling softly to himself.

"I suppose this man Vance is the former lover?" he asked.

"He is," said Gerald.

"He will depart from this sorrowful world tonight, then?"

"He will," said Gerald.

"And then," said Banti, "I shall take you and the lady of your heart away with me."

Gerald paused in his walking, then frowned upon Banti.

"Louis," he said, "let me make this clear to you: I would give up a kingdom rather than take a chance which might harm her. Carry her into an adventure like that? I had rather be burned alive."

"Really?" said Banti, arching his brows. "But, my dear Gerald, if you marry the lady, do you think that you will be able to trust yourself thereafter?"

"Louis, you have never seen her."

"To be sure. But marriage is a great blunder of good resolutions. They vanish like the rainbow under the sun. One never comes to the pot of gold. Consider yourself. Here in the full flush of a new love, Gerald, when I paint the picture of that kingdom which is waiting for you in the sea, I notice that your eyes roll and your lip twitches and your hand jumps as though you were already in the fight. And in your heart of hearts you are already down yonder in the fight, scheming, plotting, learning a Negro tongue, working your way into Negro hearts, drilling a savage army. Tush! I can see the pull on you. It almost shakes you even now. You are on the verge of saying that you will take the wife with you. But after marriage, Gerald, when time dulls the gold... what then, monsieur?"

"Then there will be no devil named Banti bringing temptations."

"I? I am only one weak ship bringing a single cargo to port. But you, Gerald! What of you? Your own mind is the fruitful hatchery of strange schemes. The love of adventure is born in the blood. It is in yours. The time will come, lad, the time will come. The good Lord watches! He will whisper into your ear of some strange land... by the pole... an oasis in the desert... a shrine in Persia... and you must be gone. The tiger cannot be tamed. It may be wounded. It may be subdued by pain and kept quiet for the moment. But when it is healed, when you are past the first pangs of love, what then, Gerald?"

"Curse you and your tongue, Louis. I'll hear no more of this!"

"You love her, do you not?"

"Like a part of heaven... like all of heaven... and she is all of it that I shall ever see."

"If there is such a thing as punishment for sin, why, yes, Gerald, she is all of it that you will see. But, if you love her, you care for her happiness more than for yours."

"A thousand times!"

"Then give her up!"

"Ah?"

"I say give her up. Come. You are capable of noble action. This will be one of them. Step out of her life while you may. Step out before you break her heart."

"Banti—"

"I shall not come back."

"No, no! I have to thrash this out with you!"

"Talk it over with yourself. You are a better judge than I!"

"Banti, stay for five minutes?"

"I shall be waiting... at eight o'clock... on the edge of the town. I shall have a horse. Bring your own. And we will ride all night into the lowlands. Remember!"

"Banti, for the sake of our friendship..."

"Adieu!"

The door closed in the face of Gerald. He leaned against it until a tumult of new thoughts rushed into his brain—things which he should have said. He tore the door open, but Banti was already out of sight, and Gerald turned slowly back into the room.

XI. — TOM WRITES A LETTER

Night came early on that Christmas Eve. The steep shadow dropped from the western peaks over the little town, and by four o'clock it was dusk, with a wild wind screaming about the hotel. It shook the crazy building. It blew a vagary of drafts through the cracks in the floor, through the cracks in the walls. But through it all Gerald lay forward on his bed with his hands over his face.

There had never been a torment like this before. Not that march across the desert when the mirage floated before them with its blue, cool promise of water—not that moment earlier in this same day when he had told the truth to Kate—nothing compared with that long time of loneliness.

If Banti had been there, if one human being had been near to argue with and convince and thereby convince himself—but there was no one, and the solitude was a terrible judge hearing his thoughts one by one and spurning them away.

He looked at his watch suddenly and saw that it was seven o'clock. In a single hour he must face poor Tom Vance in Canton Douglas's place and kill him. There would be no chance to shoot for the hip or the shoulder, for Tom Vance would himself shoot to kill his treacherous enemy, and it was life or death for Gerald.

Not that he doubted the outcome. He had met sterner men than Tom Vance and killed them. And he would drop Tom with the suddenness of mercy.

And yet his soul rebelled against it. Rather any other man he had ever met than this fellow whom he had so wronged. But suppose he could meet him and talk with him, man to man, for ten minutes, might not something be done?

He hurried out into the night, filled with the blind hope. Through the slowly falling sleet—for the wind had fallen to a whisper—he went up the street to the cabin of Tom Vance far at the end. He could look past it up the hillside to the glimmer of light in the cabin of old Maddern. In that house were the only people in the town who did not know, for the story would be kept from their ears surely.

With his hand raised to knock at the door, he hesitated. To walk in suddenly on Tom might be merely to bring to a quick head the passion which was in the young miner. There might well be a reaching for guns—and then the tragedy even earlier than he had dreaded to meet it.

Full of that thought, he went around the shack to the window on the farther side. It was sheltered by a projection of the roof and was clear of snow or frost; he could look through to the interior. There was Tom Vance not the distance of an arm's reach away!

Gerald shrank back. Then, recalling that the light inside would blind the man within to all that stood beyond the window, he came closer again. And he saw the pen scrawl slowly across the paper, hesitate, and then go on again, a painful effort.

It wasn't hard to make it out. The lantern light fell strongly upon the page, and the stub pen blotted the paper with heavy, black lines. So he read the letter with ease:

Dearest Kate:
If this comes to you, I shall be dead as you read it, and Kern shall have killed me. I have challenged him. We are to meet tonight at Douglas's place, and there will be only one ending. I know what he can do. He can almost think with a six-shooter. And, though I am a good shot, I cannot stand up to such a marksman. But I shall do my best.
I don't want you to think of me as a man who has thrown himself away as a sacrifice. I know that the chances are against me, ten to one, but the tenth chance is worth playing for. With the help of heaven, I shall kill him!
You may think that I am a hound for fighting with a man you have said you love. But once you told me that you loved me, and I believed you. And I still believe that you cared for me as much as you care for him now. But there is some sort of fascination about him. The boys have told me when they begged me to take back my challenge or else fail to appear at Canton's tonight. They have told me how he broke down the nerve of Curly. They had sworn that no one can stand up against him.
And wouldn't it be odd if a man who can break the nerve of trained fighters couldn't win over a girl just as he pleased?
That is why I'm taking the tenth chance. Not that you'll ever care for me afterwards, but because at least I'll have cleared the road for some other good man more worthy of you than either Kern or me.
I know that he is not your kind of man. He's a stranger. He talks in a new way. He thinks in a new way. He acts as no one in the mountains acts. He has a manner of fixing his eye on a person and paralyzing the mind and making one think the thoughts he wishes to put into one's head. And that's what he has done with you.
You half admitted it when you told me that you no longer cared for me because of him. When I asked you if you really loved him, you looked past me—a queer, far-away look. You seemed half afraid to answer. You would love him some day, you told me, more than you could ever love any other man.
But I think that you will never come to that day. Kate, take this letter as my warning. I am dying for the privilege of telling you what I think in honesty. And I swear to you that you can never be happy with him.
Where has he been? What has he done? Who knows his past?
Have you ever thought of asking him those questions? Has he ever spoken to you about friends of his? No, and I think he never will. One thing at least I know. I know that he is a man who has been hunted. He has a quick, sharp way of looking at new faces that come near him. Sometimes, when people pass behind him, he shivers a little. And, when he is not speaking, his mouth is set, and his teeth are locked together. He looks in repose as though he were making up his mind to do some desperate act.
I saw all these things that one evening I was with him. And I knew then that danger—hours and days and months of deadly danger—had given him those characteristics.

So, in the name of heaven, Kate, learn more about his past before you marry him. And remember this—that a man who is capable of cheating and betraying another man as he cheated and betrayed me is capable of no really good thing.
I know that you will hate me when you have read this letter. Warnings are never welcome. But because I love you, Kate, I cannot help writing. Good bye, my dear.
Tom.

So the letter came slowly to its end, and Gerald stepped back into the blanketing night and the soft whisper of the wind.

Who was it that said that truth sits upon the lips of dying men? He could not remember, but he knew the truth of all the words which Tom had written. And it was new to Gerald. Yes, the power with which he had been able to break down the wills of strong men might surely be strong enough to break down the will of a young girl. And had she, indeed, come to care for him chiefly because he was strange? He was recalled to a dozen times when he had found her looking at him half in terror, looking at him and past him as though she were seeing the future and trembling at what she saw.

Sick at heart, he came slowly back to the window. In the farther corner Tom was strapping on cartridge belt and the heavy Colt hanging in the holster. He took up a broad-brimmed, felt hat and placed it carefully on his head. Over his shoulders he threw a slicker. Next he drew out the revolver and went carefully over its action.

When he was assured that all was in working order, he dropped the gun back into its leather sheath and marched to the door.

"The fool!" muttered Gerald. "To go twenty minutes ahead of time and then stand the strain of waiting!"

But Tom was not yet ready to leave. He turned again. He hesitated with a strange, half-sad, half-bewildered look. Presently, he dropped to his knees beside his bunk. He clasped his thick, brown hands together. He raised his head, and Gerald watched the moving of his lips in prayer—words which came slowly, a long-forgotten lesson, learned at his mother's knee, was brought back to him and delivered him from the evil he would have done.

XII. — WHAT WOMEN HATE MOST

Assembled Culver City was packed into Canton Douglas's place, and yet not a dollar's worth of business had been done, except at the bar. And when the door finally opened, at three minutes before the great clock at the end of the hall showed eight, all heads jerked around and watched Tommy Vance step in.

It was noted that he was quite pale, and that his lips were compressed hard—a bad sign of the condition of his nerves. But he bore himself stiffly erect. He looked quietly over the crowd, made sure that the man he wanted was not yet come, and walked with deliberation to a seat near the clock, pulling up a chair well apart from the others. There he sat and crossed his legs and waited.

"Just like the time that Cheyenne Curly...," muttered someone.

"Except that it's different," said another. "Curly was a skunk. And Tom Vance is as white as they make 'em."

"He is," agreed another. "It's a shame that they got to have this trouble. Women sure get at the bottom of all the mischief."

"And Christmas Eve, too!"

"Is it? God damn me if I hadn't forgot that it was the twenty-fourth! Tomorrow's Christmas?"

"It sure is."

"There'll be no Christmas for poor Tom Vance this year."

"Why not? Maybe he'll have the luck against Kern."

"Luck? There ain't any luck against Kern. He's like fate. You can't get away from him. When his eye takes hold of you, you just feel that you're gone, that's all."

"There's a considerable talk about this Kern," said a grizzle-haired old-timer who was proud of being able to remember the early frontier and the men of those hardy days. "But what's he done? He scared out two low-lived bullies. And any white man that don't get scared can beat an ignorant hound that don't know nothing but picking trouble. This here will be different. This boy Vance is clean. He'll make a different kind of fight."

"If his nerve holds. Look here! He can't hardly roll a cigarette!"

Tom had ventured on this task and was dribbling tobacco wastefully over the floor. Finally, the paper tore across. He crumpled it, dropped it, and drew out the makings again.

"There you are," said the gray-haired observer. "There's the right nerve for you. He's going to try again. He'll do better this time, too. Look!"

The second cigarette was deftly and smoothly manufactured, lighted, and a cloud of smoke puffed from Tom's lips.

"That ain't nerve," said Canton himself, who was near. "That's the way a gent will act when he's facing a death sentence. He ain't got any hope. All he wants to do is to die game without showing no white feather. But why don't Kern show up? It's past time!"

Here eight o'clock began striking, the brazen chimes booming loudly through the hushed room, and when the last sound echoed away to a murmur every man leaned forward, expecting to see the door fly open. The cigarette fell from the numbed fingers of Tom Vance. But the door did not stir. And slowly the crowd settled back.

"He's waiting so's he can break Tom's nerve just the way he busted Cheyenne Curly's."

"It's a mighty poor thing to do," said Canton with heat. "I don't mind saying that it's downright low to play that sort of game with poor Tom that ain't got a chance in a hundred, anyway."

They waited five minutes, ten minutes, and the scowls of the miners grew blacker and blacker. The trick of Gerald was patent to all, and it enraged them.

"Hey, Jerry!" called Canton suddenly to one of the men who was making a pretense at continuing a card game. "Run over to the hotel, will you? Tell Gerald that his friend is waiting for him plumb anxious, will you? And tell him that he's a mile overdue!"

There was a growl of assent from a hundred throats, and Jerry went off reluctantly on an errand which might prove dangerous unless the message were phrased tenderly enough. In three minutes he came back, and he came with a rush that knocked the swinging door wide.

"Boys!" he shouted as he came to a halt, "I looked up in his room. He ain't there, and his things are gone. I run down and looked into the stable. And Sorrow wasn't there. And nobody ain't seen nothing of Kern nowhere!"

"By heaven!" roared the old-timer of the gray hair, rising from his place. "I sort of suspicioned it! He didn't like this game. He knew he had different kind of meat to chew this time! He's been bluffed out! He's quit cold, the yaller dog!"

Tumult instantly reigned in Canton's place. Out poured the hundred searchers. They swarmed through the town, but they found no trace of Gerald Kern.

"Up yonder!" called an inspired voice at last, pointing to the light in the window of the Maddern cabin. "I'll bet a thousand that he's up there sitting pretty and talking to his girl. Let's take a look!"

And up the slope they went with a willing rush. They reached the door. It was opened by Maddern, with Kate behind him.

"Where's Kern?" they demanded.

"Not here," they were told. "And what's up, boys?"

"The hound has run out on Tom Vance. He's showed yaller! He's quit without daring to show his face!"

"No, no!" cried Kate.

"Here's a hundred of us to swear to it," said Canton Douglas furiously.

And Kate raised her hands to her face.

It was hard going over the mountains. Though the wagons had beaten out a trail, it was deep with snow, and the two horsemen let their mounts labor on, giving them what aid they could to guide them until the clouds were brushed from the sky and the stars looked down to show them the way. A little later, they reached the last of the ridges. Below them spread the lowlands and a safer and an easier trail to follow.

Here they drew rein, and Gerald looked back.

"Cher ami," said Banti, "no halting by the way. The small waiting makes the great heart ache. Forward, comrade!"

"Hush, Louis. It is my last look!"

"Ah, my friend, it will be far better when you have your first look at your kingdom yonder over the sea."

"But this is my country," he said. "And this is the last time that I shall see it."

So the silence grew, while Banti gnawed his lip with anxiety.

"It is my torment if you linger here," he said gently, at last.

"Louis," murmured his friend, "what is it that a woman detests most in a man?"

"A close string drawn on the pocketbook."

"We are not in France," said Gerald with a touch of scorn. "Tell me again."

"Long silences at the table," said Banti. "They drive the poor dears mad. Yes, a silent husband is even worse than a pinched wallet."

"Still wrong," said Gerald. "What a woman hates most of all in a man is cowardice. A woman ceases to love a man who runs away from danger."

"Eh?"

"Because that is rot at the heart of the tree."

"Perhaps you are right. But what of that?"

"Nothing," said Gerald. "Let us ride on again."

They passed on down the slope. And the steady trot of the horses covered the weary miles one by one. As for Banti, he whistled; he sang; he told wild tales of a dozen lands, and all without drawing a word from his companion until, as they drew near to a town, he said:

"What is in your head now, Gerald? Tell me the thought which has stopped that restless tongue of yours so long?"

"I shall tell you," said Gerald, "though it will mean nothing to you. I have been thinking of Christmas Day, Louis, and the power of prayer."

Louis considered a moment.

"Ah, yes," he said at last. "I had forgotten. But this is Christmas, and on this day one goes back to the silly thoughts of one's childhood. Is it not so?"

Made in the USA
Charleston, SC
10 December 2015